PEDRO

PEDRO THE
GREAT

by Fran Manushkin

illustrated by
Tammie Lyon

CAPSTONE PRESS
a capstone imprint

Pedro is published by Picture Window Books,
a Capstone Imprint
1710 Roe Crest Drive
North Mankato, Minnesota 56003
www.mycapstone.com

Cataloging-in-Publication Data is available on the Library of Congress website.

ISBN: 978-1-5158-1913-4

Summary: Join Pedro for his latest adventures with his pal Katie Woo. One day,
he's pretending he's a pirate, sailing the high seas. The next day, he's practicing
his karate, being as fierce as a ninja star. But no matter what adventure Pedro's
having, he's always Pedro the Great!

Designer: Tracy McCabe

Design Elements: Shutterstock

Photo Credit:
Tammie Lyon, pg. 96

Printed and bound in the USA.
010368F17

To: GUS
From: Meemers & Gramps

Table of Contents

PIRATE
PEDRO

"Ahoy there! Wake up!" said Pedro's dad. "It's Pirate Day at school."

Pedro got up fast.

He ate his pirate pancakes and put on his pirate hat.

"Good-bye," Pedro said. "See you later, landlubbers!"

"Take me along!"
said Paco.

"You are
too little," said
Pedro.

Peppy, Pedro's
puppy, tried to come
too.

"No way!"
said Pedro.
"Puppies can't
be pirates."

At school, Miss Winkle said, "Hello, crew! Are you ready to be pirates?"

"Arrr!" yelled Pedro and Katie and JoJo.

"Can you unscramble
these pirate words?" asked Miss
Winkle.

"*Glaf* is flag!" said
Pedro. "And *words* is sword!"

"Righto!" said Miss Winkle.

During art, Pedro made a pirate flag.

"It's called a Jolly Roger," said Katie. "They named it after a happy man named Roger."

JoJo told the class a story about a girl pirate.

"Her name was Mary Read," said JoJo. "She was fierce!"

After school, Pedro said, "Let's be pirates at my house."

"Arrr!" yelled Katie. "I'll be the captain. I'm fierce — just like Mary Read!"

"No way!" said Pedro. "Being captain is my job."

Pedro's clubhouse was their
ship. He proudly put up the Jolly
Roger.

"I want to be a pirate too!"
yelled Paco. He put on an eye
patch and began running around.

"Watch out!" warned JoJo.

"You are walking the plank!"

JoJo grabbed Paco before he fell overboard!

"I think fast," JoJo bragged. "That's why I should be the captain."

"No! I should be captain,"
said Katie. "I have sharper eyes.
I can see a crow sitting on our
crow's nest."

"But I am strong," said Pedro. "And brave! See my sword? I can win any fight!"

Suddenly, it began to rain.

"Don't worry," said Pedro. "My ship is strong! It will keep us dry through any storm."

Below the ship, Peppy was rolling in the mud.

Oops! Pedro dropped his sword — into the puddle.

Peppy picked it up to fetch it.
He was a good fetcher.

"No!" yelled Pedro. "It is not a
stick. Don't bring it back to me."

Did Peppy listen? No! He climbed the ladder and shook mud all over the pirates!

"Shiver me timbers!" shouted
Pedro. "It's fun getting wet!"

"For sure!" yelled Katie,
laughing.

"Yes!" said JoJo. "We are jolly
pirates."

"We would all be jolly captains," said Pedro. "Maybe we should take turns."

"I thought of that too," said Katie.

"So did I!" said JoJo.

Soon it was time for a snack of hot dogs and pirate grog.

All the pirates agreed: it was very tasty!

PEDRO AND THE
SHARK

Pedro told his dad, "I'm doing something fishy today."

"You are?" asked his dad.

"Yes!" Pedro smiled. "I'm going to the aquarium."

His dad laughed. "That *is* fishy!"

"I've saved some money," said Pedro. "I'm bringing back a souvenir."

"Great!" said his dad. "I can't wait to see it."

At the aquarium, Miss Winkle told the class, "Be sure to stay together."

"That's easy," said Pedro. "We can pretend we are minnows. They always stick together."

"It's cool in here," said Katie, "and dark."

"Yes," added JoJo. "It's a little spooky."

"Here comes something crabby!" said Pedro.

"Is it my baby brother?" joked Barry.

"Very funny!" said Miss Winkle. "It's a hermit crab."

"I love the starfish," said Katie. "They look dreamy."

"But the jellyfish looks lonely," said JoJo. "Maybe he's looking for a peanut butter fish."

"I'd love to take a ride on
the sea horse," said Pedro. "But I
would need to be smaller."

"Yes," said Katie. "And don't
forget your snorkel!"

Roddy ran ahead. "YAY!" he yelled. "Here come the sharks! *Duck!*"

"Yikes!" said Pedro. "Those teeth look sharp. I don't want to ride on *him.*"

"You know," said Pedro, "all this water is making me thirsty."

He walked away to find a water fountain.

When Pedro finished drinking, he looked for his class. They were gone.

Pedro was alone — with the shark!

"See you later!" Pedro yelled. "I have to find my class."

"Here they are!" He smiled. "I see JoJo!"

No! It wasn't her.

"I bet my class is around this corner," said Pedro.

The room was dark and filled with whales.

"Yay!" yelled Pedro. "Here's my class."

No! It *wasn't*! Pedro ran this way and that way, but he kept coming back to the shark.

Pedro looked at the shark, who was swimming in circles.

"Ha!" Pedro smiled. "That's why I can't find my class! I've been going in circles. Thanks for the clue."

Pedro tried a new direction.

He passed a sea turtle. She moved slowly, looking calm and wise.

"I'll try that," said Pedro.

Pedro took a deep breath.

He walked slowly. "I'll turn left this time, then right."

Success! Pedro found his class.

"Here you are!" said Miss Winkle. "We were going to start searching."

"I found you first," Pedro said proudly.

When he got home, Pedro said,
"Dad, come see my souvenirs."

His dad smiled, "Why did you
choose a shark and a sea turtle?"

"It's a long story," said Pedro.

"Good," said his dad. "You can tell me while we walk Peppy."

Pedro's story was so long, they walked around the block twice.

"Sometimes," said Pedro, "it's fun to go in circles."

And it was!

PEDRO'S TRICKY
TOWER

Pedro loved to build. He helped his father make a tree house. He helped his grandpa build a fireplace.

One day, his teacher, Miss
Winkle, told the class, "I have a
tricky building project for you."

"Yay!" yelled Roddy. "I love tricks. I play them on people all the time."

"That's not the kind of *tricky* I mean," said Miss Winkle. "We are going to try to build the tallest tower."

"That's easy!" bragged Pedro.

"All we need are lots of bricks."

"We are not using bricks,"
said Miss Winkle. "We are using
nineteen paper cups. You will be
working in teams."

Barry and JoJo were on Katie Woo's team. Sophie was on Pedro's team. So was Roddy!

"Watch out!" warned Katie.

"R-O-D-D-Y spells T-R-O-U-B-L-E."

Miss Winkle told the teams,
"Before you build, you need
to plan."

"I don't need to plan," said
Pedro. "I know what to do."

Pedro began piling up paper cups. He tried to build high, but the towers kept falling down.

Roddy put four paper cups on his head.

"Watch out!" he joked. "My towers are falling down too."

Pedro and Sophie tried again and again. But the cups kept falling.

"Oh, boy!" said Pedro. "I wish we had some bricks."

Then it was time for recess.

Roddy told Pedro, "Forget the
tower! Let's see who can do the
most handstands. I know I'll win!"

Roddy flipped upside down and back again. Pedro tried it. He kept falling down.

"Watch me and learn," said Roddy.

Pedro did watch Roddy.

Then he began thinking.

"That's it!" Pedro yelled. "You showed me how to build the tallest tower."

After recess, Pedro ran back to class. He said, "Let's put some of the cups right side up and some upside down."

Pedro and Sophie began to build.

"Let me help," said Roddy. He began piling up the cups.

Their tower got higher and higher. It did not fall! It was the tallest tower!

"Way to go!" said Miss Winkle.

Roddy couldn't stop smiling.

He told Pedro, "I knew we could

do it!"

He gave Pedro a high five.

After school, Pedro said, "Want to help me fix my tree house?"

"Cool!" said Roddy. "I'll race you there."

They both won.

PEDRO THE
NINJA

Pedro and Paco were watching
a ninja cartoon.

"Wow!" said Paco. "That kick
was awesome."

"I want to be in a ninja
movie," said Pedro.

He yelled, "Hi-YA!"

Oops! Pedro kicked a chair.

"Ouch!" he said. "Being a
ninja is tricky."

"I can help you," said Pedro's dad. "Would you like to take karate lessons?"

"For sure!" said Pedro.

His dad got Pedro a robe called a *gi*. "Wow!" Pedro said. "I look cool!"

"You do!" said Paco. "I wish I could go to class."

"Maybe next year," said his dad.

JoJo and Katie were in Pedro's class. Everyone bowed to the teacher, Sensei Kono.

He said, "The first thing you will learn is this stance."

Pedro did the stance over
and over. He told JoJo, "I feel
like a statue."

"But you look fierce,"
said Katie.

At the next class, Sensei Kono showed them the side kick.

It was tricky. It took balance and lots of practice.

Pedro loved side kicking! He showed Paco how to do it.

Peppy tried it too. He kicked over his food bowl.

Every day after school, Pedro and his friends pretended they were in a ninja movie.

"Let's practice our kicks," said JoJo.

Oops! She kicked a tree and apples began falling — toward Paco's head!

"Hi-YA!" yelled Pedro, blocking the apples.

"Cool moves!" said Katie.

"I'm almost a ninja star," said Pedro. "It won't be long!"

Punches were the most fun.

Pedro punched beach balls and
balloons.

Pop! Pop! Pop!

No more balloons.

Pedro told Paco, "Ninja stars are always sneaky."

Pedro practiced being sneaky by trying to grab cookies before supper.

"Hi-YA!" yelled his mom.

"Caught you!"

She was sneaky too.

Pedro and Paco played ninja in their room.

"Hi-YA!" Pedro yelled, jumping out of the closet.

Paco screamed and laughed.

"You know," Pedro told Paco,
"we are having so much fun, it's
okay if we aren't ninja movie
stars."

"Is that so?" said their dad.

The next day, Pedro's friends came over to see a new ninja movie.

"This is a great one," said Pedro's mom.

"I'll say!" His dad winked.

Surprise! The ninjas were Pedro and his friends!

Pedro's dad was sneaky. While they were doing karate, he was making action videos.

"We didn't look too fierce at the start," said Pedro.

"Right!" said Katie. "But we got better and better."

"We are the coolest," said Pedro.

"We are ninja stars," said JoJo.

"Hi-YA!" they yelled.

And they all took a bow.

JOKE AROUND

★ What is a pirate's
favorite animal?
an arrrrrrdvark

★ When is the best time for a pirate
to buy his shop?
when it's on sail

★ Why did the pirate buy an
eye patch?
He didn't have enough money
for an iPad.

★ Why can't pirates
play cards?
They are sitting
on the deck.

★ What is a shark's
favorite candy?
jaw breakers

★ Why won't the shrimp
share its toys?
Because it's shellfish.

★ Why did the shark cross the road?
to get to the other tide

★ What is the most famous
fish in the ocean?
the starfish

JOKE AROUND

★ What kind of nails do carpenters hate to hammer?
fingernails

★ Why did the carpenter fall asleep on the job?
He was board.

★ What is the tallest tower in town?
the library — it has lots of stories

★ What animal can jump higher than Pedro's tower?
any animal — the tower can't jump

WITH PEDRO!

★ What is the ninja's favorite seafood?
swordfish

★ What do ninjas say when they see you?
"Hi-YA!"

★ What do ninjas drink during the summer?
kara-TEA

★ What football position do ninjas like most?
kicker

About the Author

Fran Manushkin is the author
of many popular picture books,
including *Happy in Our Skin*;
Baby, Come Out!; *Latkes and
Applesauce: A Hanukkah Story*;
The Tushy Book; *The Belly Book*;
and *Big Girl Panties*. Fran writes
on her beloved Mac computer in New York City,
without the help of her two naughty cats, Chaim
and Goldy.

About the Illustrator

Tammie Lyon began her love for
drawing at a young age while sitting
at the kitchen table with her dad.
She continued her love of art and
eventually attended the Columbus
College of Art and Design, where she
earned a bachelor's degree in fine
art. After a brief career as a professional ballet dancer, she
decided to devote herself full time to illustration. Today
she lives with her husband, Lee, in Cincinnati, Ohio. Her
dogs, Gus and Dudley, keep her company as she works in
her studio.